12

books by
Shigeo Watanabe and Yasuo Ohtomo

I Can Do It All By Myself books

How do I put it on?
An American Library Association
Notable Children's Book

What a good lunch!

Get set! Go!

I'm king of the castle!

I can ride it!

Where's my daddy?

I can build a house!

I can take a walk!

I Love To Do Things With Daddy books

Daddy, play with me!

I can take a bath!

I can take a bath!

Shigeo Watanabe   Pictures by Yasuo Ohtomo

PHILOMEL BOOKS

Look at me, I'm covered with sand!

Oh, no, I don't want a bath!

Come along!

Daddy's having
a bath, too.

Ooh, the water tickles.

This is fun.

Daddy's scrubbing my back.

Now it's my turn to scrub.

Watch out, Daddy!
I'm a submarine.

I took a bath with Daddy.

I can put
these on
all by myself.

We're all nice and clean now.

I love to do things with Daddy.

Library of Congress Cataloging-in-Publication Data
Watanabe, Shigeo, 1928–   I can take a bath!.
Originally published: Mammy, I took a bath
with daddy. Summary: A young bear is
reluctant to take a bath until he
gets into the tub with his father
and they have fun together.
[1. Bears—Fiction.   2. Baths—Fiction.
3. Fathers and sons—Fiction]
1. Otomo, Yasuo, ill.   II. Title.
PZ7.W2615Iak   1987   [E]   86-5080
ISBN 0-399-21362-7